Enough is Enough!

Caroline peeked at the picture Duncan had drawn. It was a skinny person with a big head and an ugly dog face. It had a long pointed nose and fangs and enormous drooping ears. And underneath, Duncan had scrawled, *Caroline Zucker*.

Caroline gasped and touched her twin pony-tails. Did they really look like floppy dog ears?

"Duncan, you . . . *rat*," she hissed. When his shoulders started to shake, Caroline knew he was laughing at her.

She sat back in her chair and wrinkled her nose, trying to hold back her tears. She wasn't a crybaby — Caroline knew these were *mad* tears. Duncan Fairbush was the meanest boy in the whole school! One of these days, she was going to get back at him. Then he'd be sorry he'd ever made fun of Caroline Zucker!

Look for these books in the Caroline Zucker series:

Caroline Zucker Gets Even

Caroline Zucker Meets Her Match

Caroline Zucker Gets Her Wish

Caroline Zucker and The Birthday Disaster

Caroline Zucker Makes a Big Mistake

Caroline Zucker Helps Out

Caroline Zucker
Gets Even

by Jan Bradford

Illustrated by Marcy Ramsey

Troll Associates

Library of Congress Cataloging-in-Publication Data

Bradford, Jan.
  Caroline Zucker gets even / by Jan Bradford; illustrated by Marcy
Dunn Ramsey.
     p.   cm.
  Summary: Caroline and her best friend Maria plot to outwit Duncan,
the most obnoxious boy in their third grade class.
  ISBN 0-8167-2015-0 (lib. bdg.)   ISBN 0-8167-2016-9 (pbk.)
  [1. Schools—Fiction.   2. Friendship—Fiction.]   I. Ramsey, Marcy
Dunn, ill.   II. Title.
PZ7.B7228Car   1991
[Fic]—dc20   89-20630

A TROLL BOOK, published by Troll Associates

1

CAN A BAD DAY GET WORSE?

"Do you all understand how to do your book reports?"

Caroline Zucker nodded. She couldn't wait to get started. Finally, she had an idea that was guaranteed to make her third-grade teacher like her. Mrs. Nicks was going to be impressed.

The teacher clapped her hands as she did every day at eleven-fifty. "Since there are no questions, let's line up for lunch."

Caroline opened her desk to search for her lunch ticket. Just then, Duncan Fairbush jumped out of his seat. His chair knocked back against Caroline's desk and she had to grab the

desk top with both hands to keep it from falling on her head.

"Watch it!" she told him. "You could have *decapitated* me."

Caroline smiled to herself. She had heard the word on television last night, but she doubted Duncan would know that *decapitate* meant cutting off someone's head. He was such a jerk.

Caroline stood up and stuffed her lunch ticket into the pocket of her brown corduroy pants. She grinned at her best friend, Maria Santiago. "I'm starving."

"I hope Fairbush doesn't eat everything before it's our turn," Maria complained as the line started moving into the hall.

"Don't worry." Caroline giggled. "We're having pizza today. Remember the last time he ate pizza? He started scratching himself all over in the middle of math because he's allergic to tomatoes." Although Caroline could hear her mother saying it wasn't nice to make fun of people, she told herself Duncan Fairbush didn't count. He wasn't really human.

They stood in line for their pizza slices and milk cartons and then followed their class into the lunchroom. Caroline and Maria squeezed between Samantha Collins and Kevin Sutton, who was busy picking all the pepperoni off his pizza.

"I can't wait to start my book report," Caroline told her friend.

"Are you crazy?" Maria looked up and down the table as if she was worried someone else had heard Caroline. "*No one* admits they want to do a book report."

"But I have a plan. Mrs. Nicks is going to love my . . . " Caroline leaned close to Maria so no one else would hear, ". . . my diorama."

"Diorama?" Maria whispered.

"Yes. I'm going to read *Little House in the Big Woods*. And I'm going to make a diorama of the inside of the Ingalls's cabin!" Mrs. Nicks talked about Laura Ingalls Wilder, the author of the book, so much that she made it sound as if they were personal friends. But Caroline knew the real Laura had lived a long time ago.

Caroline leaned back, feeling very pleased. At last, Mrs. Nicks would have to notice that she was special. When the teacher got tired of reading everyone else's boring old book reports, she would really appreciate Caroline's work.

Maria shook her head. "You're so smart, Caroline Zucker! I wish I'd thought of doing a diorama."

"Maybe we could do it together," Caroline said. "Mrs. Nicks never said it couldn't be a team project."

"No, it's your idea."

Caroline loved the way Maria was always fair. Caroline's own sisters would probably steal the idea if they were in third grade, but they weren't. They always "borrowed" her colored markers without asking and then gave them back after they were dried-out and useless.

"Oh, no . . . " Maria's worried voice interrupted Caroline's thoughts. "You dripped tomato sauce on your shirt!"

Caroline had to cross her eyes to look down at her front. Maria was right. There was a red stain on her chest. "I'll have to hide this before my mom sees it."

Maria nodded. "You're right. If she sees it, she'll say how lucky it was you weren't wearing pink — "

"Or lavender or light blue," Caroline said with

a sigh. Her mother kept telling her it was more sensible for a busy third-grader to wear dark clothes. When she was old enough to buy her own clothes, Caroline was going to have closets full of pink and lavender skirts and dresses. She would have so many clothes that it wouldn't matter if something got dirty. She'd just throw it away!

After dinner that night, Caroline slid down into the couch cushions and tried to concentrate on *Little House in the Big Woods*. But she hadn't counted on Patricia's piano practice. "Hey, I'm trying to read!" she yelled.

Her six-year-old sister stopped playing scales long enough to say, "I have to practice."

"Can't you do it later?"

"No. *Mom!*" Patricia's blue eyes filled with tears as their mother hurried into the room.

"What's going on here?" Mrs. Zucker asked both girls.

"Caroline won't let me practice. And you know how important it is. . . ."

Caroline thought she would gag if her sister started repeating the things Miss Church, the piano teacher, liked to say. Patricia had only started taking lessons last year. Their parents had even bought her a piano just because Miss Church had made the mistake of saying Patricia was talented. And Patricia wasn't going to let anyone forget it.

"Have you been bothering your sister?" Caroline's mother asked.

"No." Caroline shoved her hands into her pockets. "*She* was bothering *me*."

"You were just reading a dumb book," Patricia said from the piano bench.

"My school work is more important than your dumb scales!"

"Caroline!"

Caroline stuck out her chin to make what her mother called her stubborn face. She heard soft footsteps and knew her youngest sister, Vicki, was sneaking into the room. She didn't need someone in kindergarten to join the Pick-On-Caroline club, so she ignored her, hoping she'd go away.

Caroline got her book and showed it to her mother. "I have to read this before I can do my project."

"*Little House in the Big Woods.*" Her mother nodded. "That's a good book. I think you'll like it."

"And Mrs. Nicks is going to love my diorama. I just know she's finally going to like me."

Her mother sighed. "I thought we had settled this. Mrs. Nicks doesn't dislike you."

"Yes she does." Her mother wasn't at school day after day to see the way Mrs. Nicks treated Caroline. "She never says how well I read aloud, even though no one else can read as good. And she *never* tries to stop Duncan Fairbush from bugging me."

"I'm sure she notices you, but she has twenty-eight other students to watch, too. You're a big girl now," her mother reminded her. "And growing up means learning to adjust to changes."

"But I don't want to have a mean teacher."

Her mother shook her head. "She isn't mean. Your father and I have explained that you're lucky to have a teacher who doesn't play favorites."

"But Duncan Fairbush is such a jerk! Today he nearly slammed my desk top down on my head!"

"It looks like you survived." Her mother pressed her lips together, trying not to laugh. Why did grownups think kid disasters were so funny?

"You won't be laughing when they call to tell you Duncan Fairbush decapitated me!"

Her mother had to put her hand over her mouth to hide her smile. "Caroline, I just can't believe third grade is as terrible as you're making it sound. You'll have to get used to it."

Caroline tucked Laura Ingalls Wilder under her arm and stomped up the stairs to her room under the eaves.

When her mother had first started working lots of different shifts at the hospital, Caroline had thought it would be fun to be in charge of her sisters . . . to be more grown-up. And then she learned being *grown-up* meant starting dinner, and walking the dog, and folding the wash. And she didn't even get to boss her sisters around, because Laurie Morrell, one of her father's high-school students, came to the house after school and stayed there until one of their parents came home. Now, *growing up* meant suffering through a year with Mrs. Nicks

9

and Duncan Fairbush without getting any help from anybody. It wasn't fair!

She peered into her goldfish bowl and sighed. "Justin and Esmerelda, you're lucky you're just fish."

2

THE AMAZING DOG-FACED GIRL

"Class!" Mrs. Nicks called out loudly. "I know it's near the end of the day, but we still have work to do here."

Caroline had already finished all her math problems — at least the ones she could figure out. In front of her, Duncan's blond head was bent over his desk. He seemed very interested in whatever he was doing.

She slid to the very edge of her chair and leaned forward. Without standing, she strained to look over Duncan's shoulder, but she couldn't see anything.

"All right. Time's up," Mrs. Nicks announced. "Will everyone please pass their papers to the front of their row?"

Caroline heard something rustling behind her and reached back for the test copies. She hurried to pass the papers along to Duncan, but he was too busy drawing to take them from her so she hit him on the shoulder.

He spun around. "Hey, Zucker — " Before he could say something dumb and rude, she shoved the papers in his face. Duncan took a second to glare at her before he handed the tests to the person in front of him.

Duncan made a big deal about leaning over to pick up something under his desk. Caroline lifted up from her chair to peek at the picture. It was a skinny person with a big head and an ugly dog face. It had a long pointed nose, and fangs, and enormous drooping ears. And underneath, Duncan had scrawled: *Caroline Zucker.*

She gasped. He had named the gross creature after her! She touched her twin ponytails. Did they really look like floppy dog ears? She had felt so special that morning when her mother helped her fix her hair. She had even tied a red ribbon around each "tail."

"Duncan, you . . . *rat*," she hissed. She couldn't think of a better word that she wouldn't be too embarrassed to say. When his shoulders started to shake, Caroline knew he was laughing at her.

She sat back in her chair and wrinkled her nose, trying to stop the tears that were building up behind her eyes. She wasn't a crybaby — Caroline knew these were *mad* tears. Duncan Fairbush was the meanest boy in all of Hart Elementary!

Someone knocked at the door, and Mrs. Nicks stepped into the hall to talk with her visitor. As soon as she was out of the room, Duncan yelled, "Hey, Michael!"

Michael Hopkins sat in the row on the other side of Maria. In Caroline's opinion, he was the nicest boy in the whole third grade. He was smart and funny, and she liked the space that showed between his front teeth when he smiled. Michael turned toward Duncan, and so did Maria. As soon as he had their attention, Duncan held up his drawing. Maria's dark eyes opened wide and she covered her mouth.

Michael grinned, showing off the wonderful gap between his teeth, and then he said, "All right, Fairbush! Can I have it?"

"Sure." Duncan delivered the picture in person. "Want me to autograph it?"

"Yeah!"

Mrs. Nicks came back into the room, and Duncan hurried to his own desk. Later, when the teacher was erasing the blackboard, Maria passed a note to Caroline. She carefully unfolded the paper once it was hidden in her lap, under her desk. She smiled at Maria's words: *Just ten more minutes. Then we'll have our meeting at my house. No Duncans allowed!*

"The Double Club is now in session," Maria announced. Since they didn't have an official gavel, she tapped the kitchen table with a wooden spoon.

Caroline knew exactly what the first order of business was. "Let's eat!"

Maria got glasses and ice for soft drinks and Caroline raided the cookie jar. She and Maria had formed the club because they weren't old

14

enough to join the Blue Jays and go on field trips after school. It wasn't fair that they were left out just because they weren't in fourth grade yet.

They each carried their drinks to the kitchen table. The top of the table was made of glass. Caroline loved sitting there because she could look through it and see her feet.

After she checked that her shoes were tied, she said, "You know what I wish?"

Maria squinted and thought hard. "A horse. I bet you want a horse."

"No." Caroline shook her head. "I wish Duncan's family would move to Australia!"

Maria frowned. "That picture was terrible. Isn't Duncan Fairbush the meanest person you know?"

"Worse."

"What's worse than being the meanest person?"

"Being Duncan Fairbush!" Caroline giggled.

Maria laughed, too, but then she said, "Who wants to talk about him anyway? Want to listen to my new rock tape?"

"All right!" They raced through the living room

and up the curved staircase.

"What is this?" Maria's mother called from the top of the stairs. "A herd of elephants?"

"It's just us," Maria said when they stopped to catch their breath.

Caroline looked up at the tall dark-haired woman. "Hi, Mrs. Santiago."

"Hello, Caroline." Maria's mother smiled and tugged on one of the red-ribboned ponytails. "You look very nice today."

Caroline smiled back, thinking how nice Maria's mother was. Once, when Caroline had been complaining about her skinny face, Mrs. Santiago had said she had wonderful cheekbones and that she would be beautiful when she grew up.

"We're going to my room," Maria told her mother.

"We'll try not to get too loud," Caroline promised.

Maria was so lucky to have a mom who worked at home at least part of the time. Mrs. Santiago was able to bring her work home because she designed costumes for the Stratford Theater. Caroline wished her own mother could be home more instead of spending so much time working at the hospital.

They hustled into Maria's bedroom and Caroline flopped on the bed. She loved staring up at the skylight. Today, Caroline could see some clouds floating past. She sighed.

"What's wrong?" Maria asked.

"I wish I could have this room in my house."

"And I wish I had *your* neat room tucked up in the attic," Maria told her. "It's so cozy."

"Maybe if I had a lock on my door to keep my sisters out," Caroline thought aloud.

"I'd never do that. It's fun to have company." Maria put her Lucy Hanson tape into the cassette player and Caroline sat up. Lucy was eighteen and already a big star. The girls liked the way she dressed, but they liked her songs even better.

"I want to fly like a dove. I want to drift on the wind . . . " Both girls sang along with the tape. When Maria started to snap her fingers and dance, Caroline jumped off the bed to join her.

Maria danced over to her dresser and opened her jewelry box. She grabbed a pair of sparkling pierced earrings for herself and long, dangly clip-on ones for Caroline that Mrs. Santiago had found at an estate sale. "Hurry!" Maria cried. "It's almost time for 'Diamonds.'"

Caroline got the earrings on just as the song began. Maria threw a pencil to her, and Caroline knew what to do with it. They both lifted the pencil-microphones to their lips and mouthed the words to their most favorite song in the world.

"Nothing sparkles like diamonds . . . " Maria touched her earrings, even though the sparkle in them came from cut glass.

Caroline closed her eyes and tried to look emotional as she mouthed the next line. "You can't fool me, I can always spot a fake . . . "

They took turns "singing" almost the whole song until Maria threw her head back and raised her eyebrows to imitate Lucy holding a very high note. Then she fell to the floor, gasping, "Help me, Caroline! I can't breathe!"

Caroline started giggling so hard that she dropped her microphone. Every time they acted out the song, Maria had a new trick. She wanted to be an actress when she grew up and Caroline couldn't think of anyone who would make a better star.

Maria sat up and pouted. "Fine best friend you are, Zucker. What if I'd really run out of air?"

"I would have . . . " Caroline thought a minute. "I would have gotten your mom."

Maria grinned and reached for the rewind button on her cassette player. "Want to try it again?"

Caroline scrambled to find her microphone. When she pulled it out from under Maria's rose-colored bedspread, she said, "I'm ready!"

And they did it all over again.

3

"YUCKER" RHYMES WITH "ZUCKER"

"Shut up!" Duncan growled from his seat in front of Caroline.

"Sorry." She hadn't realized she was humming out loud. Mrs. Nicks had given them some free time to catch up on whatever work needed doing.

Maria was finishing her math assignment. Duncan was scribbling on a sheet of paper — Caroline hoped he wasn't doing another portrait of her! Most kids were reading books.

Caroline was working on her book report. The plans for her diorama were shaping up very

20

well. And it was Wednesday afternoon. That meant the week was half over. It was just too nice a day to worry about Duncan. She continued to hum inside her head as she sketched.

She knew exactly what she would use for the diorama. Her father had bought new shoes, and his shoe box would be perfect. She would cut a piece from the lid to make the second floor in the little house — the attic where Laura and Mary liked to play on rainy days. Another piece from the lid would divide the bedroom from the big room on the main floor. She would cut out a back door that could open and close, and windows, too.

The tricky part would be the furniture. A trundle bed. A rocking chair. A cook stove. It was going to take some thought, but Caroline liked that kind of work. Thinking and planning were fun, much more fun than just writing a report.

Caroline closed her eyes and let herself imagine the finished diorama. It was going to be wonderful! "No-Nonsense Nicks" was finally going to smile at her.

Duncan peered over his shoulder and Caroline quickly covered her sketches with her hands.

"I'm drawing again today," he said with a nasty smile that made Caroline want to gag. "Would you like to see it?"

"No!"

"I'll show it to you anyway."

Duncan turned around in his seat and set the paper on her desk. But he kept his hands on each side of the drawing so she couldn't rip it to pieces. It was a drawing of a long, skinny ant. She looked up at him. "So?"

"Check the title."

Her gaze dropped to the bottom of the sheet. It said: *Ant Yucker.*

"Isn't it funny?" he asked. "Yucker rhymes with Zucker. And you look like an ant with your dumb dark clothes and your buggy eyes!"

"Get it off my desk!" Caroline hissed.

"I'll move it if you give me a quarter."

"Knock it off, Fairbush!"

"Caroline! Duncan! Is that conversation necessary?" Mrs. Nicks asked sharply.

Duncan grabbed his picture and turned back to his own desk. Caroline sighed. She should have known they would both get in trouble. Why wouldn't her parents believe that Duncan's one goal in life was to make her miserable?

Then she noticed her diorama sketch and smiled. Her project was going to be great. And Mrs. Nicks wasn't the only one who would be impressed. For once, Duncan wouldn't be talking about bug eyes or dog ears — he'd be wishing he had thought of doing something as clever as her diorama!

"Do you think I have buggy eyes?" she asked Maria as the class went outside for recess.

Maria stared at her. "Of course not."

"Well, Duncan said I look like an ant and then he made fun of my eyes."

Maria shrugged her shoulders. "Who can understand Duncan? He's got problems."

"Maybe." Until today, Caroline had always liked her eyes. Her younger sister Patricia made a big deal about being the only one in the family with blue eyes, but Caroline was glad hers were brown. And they were big, with long lashes.

Maria punched her in the arm. "You look fine. Want to jump rope?"

"Yeah." Caroline hoped concentrating on jumping would make her stop worrying about looking like an ant.

They grabbed one of the last ropes in the box by the door. Then they ran to an empty spot in the playground behind the school. Maria jumped first. She did it twelve times before the rope tripped her. She handed it to Caroline. "Your turn."

Caroline whipped the red-and-white-striped rope over her head, and as it came down it tangled around her ankles. Not far away, she heard a familiar snort. She didn't have to look over her shoulder to know Duncan was laughing at her.

"Could I try it again?" she asked Maria.

"Sure. Show him you're not a klutz."

Caroline got the rope flying so fast a person could hardly see it. "Twenty-three, twenty-four, twenty-five."

"Now try doubles," Maria cried, clapping her hands. Their game was to do twenty-five jumps and then try to do twenty-five more, this time bouncing twice before the rope came around again.

"Nine, ten . . . *oooh!*" Caroline lost her balance and fell forward, waving her arms in the air to keep from falling on her face.

"Yucker's trying to fly!" Duncan shouted and heads turned to stare at her.

Caroline felt her face heating up. She whispered to Maria, "Am I getting red?"

Like a true best friend, Maria said, "You're just a little pink."

"It's your turn," Caroline said, staring at the ground as she held out the rope to her friend.

"Thank you!" Duncan shouted as he streaked between the two girls, grabbing the rope.

"He took our jump rope!" Maria cried in disbelief.

"I'll get it back," Caroline promised.

She raced after Duncan through the playground. He was holding the jump rope high over his head and running as fast as he could. He began to dash around the groups of kids playing games. He circled the hopscotch area and then ran between two boys playing catch. Caroline kept her eyes on him. She had to get the jump rope back.

"*Ow!*" Caroline felt something crash into her

side. Pain shot through her arm as a small girl stumbled backward, rubbing her forehead. Then the small girl started crying loudly.

Mrs. Nicks came charging in their direction. Although Caroline had stayed pretty cheerful in spite of Duncan's Ant Yucker drawing, this was too much. This was the first time she'd had a problem during recess, and it had to happen on the day Mrs. Nicks had yard duty! She was in trouble. Big trouble.

"Caroline Zucker!" No-Nonsense Nicks was making clucking sounds with her tongue as she got closer.

"Mrs. Nicks," she said, trying very hard to sound brave. "I can explain — "

"How can you possibly explain hurting a younger child? What grade are you in, dear?" she asked the little girl who was wiping her nose with her hand.

She sniffed. "First grade."

Mrs. Nicks shook her head. "Fighting with a first-grader. Whatever got into you, Caroline?"

"I was chasing the guy who stole our rope. . . ." The stern look on Mrs. Nicks's face made Caroline stop.

"Have you apologized?"

Apologize? That first-grader ran into me, Caroline told herself. Still, one more steely look from Mrs. Nicks made her change her mind. Looking down at the little girl, who now had a red mark on her forehead, Caroline whispered, "I'm sorry."

"Well, that's a start." Mrs. Nicks put her hand on Caroline's shoulder. "Now we'll go back to the classroom and talk about your detention."

Detention! Detention in Caroline's class was one of the most embarrassing things that could happen.

Caroline knew she was going to cry unless she did something to stop it. She sniffed, wishing her mother could somehow fix this mess for her.

Then she saw Duncan and Michael huddled together by the school doors. Duncan was pointing at her and both boys were grinning. She heard Duncan say, "Old Yucker's really in trouble now."

Mrs. Nicks pulled a tissue from inside her

28

sleeve. "Do you need this?"

"No, thank you." Caroline held her chin up. There was no way she was going to let the boys see her cry.

Once she and Mrs. Nicks were inside, Caroline decided it would be a good time to explain her side of the story. After all, she hadn't hurt the first-grader on purpose. She began to say, "I was just trying to get back the — "

"Miss Zucker." The teacher frowned at Caroline. "You're not going to talk your way out of detention."

Caroline should have known better than to think No-Nonsense Nicks would listen to her. She tried to look on the bright side.

Suddenly, she grinned. This afternoon, Patricia and Vicki would have to walk Baxter, the family dog, and fold the wash all by themselves while Caroline stayed after school!

4

DOUBLE CLUB TO THE RESCUE

"Friday!" Caroline tossed her light jacket into the air. She had needed it on the way to school in the morning, but the afternoon sun was warm.

"And Double Club at your house!" Maria said happily. As the girls walked up the sidewalk from the bus stop, Caroline wondered for the hundredth time why Maria seemed to love coming home with her. The Santiagos had a big house in a neighborhood full of big houses. It wasn't that Caroline didn't like living on Hawthorne Street, where the houses were old and medium-sized. She just couldn't imagine why Maria wouldn't rather have the meetings at her own house, where there weren't two little sisters spying on them all the time.

"My mom is working this afternoon," Caroline told her friend.

"I think it's neat she's a nurse."

"Yeah. But I miss seeing her when I get home from school. And today, my dad's cross-country team has a meet, so Laurie will be baby-sitting."

"I like her," Maria said. Of course, Maria rarely admitted she didn't like someone.

"She's okay." Mostly, Laurie took care of Patricia and five-year-old Vicki. But on days when Caroline wanted company, Laurie didn't mind spending time with her.

They followed the sidewalk around to the back of the house and Caroline opened the door to the kitchen. "Laurie?"

They heard Baxter racing down the stairs to greet them before they ever saw him. The sheepdog-and-something-else mutt turned the corner and slid across the kitchen floor.

He stopped at Caroline's feet and tipped his head so she could scratch him behind one ear.

"Need a walk?" Sometimes it was a pain to walk him after school, but it wasn't so bad when Maria came along.

"Hi, Caroline and Maria," Laurie said as she came into the kitchen. "Baxter sure seems happy to see you. Are you taking him out?"

"Yes," Caroline said.

"Then I'll get some treats ready for you while you're gone," Laurie told them, running a hand through her short, curly blond hair.

"Thanks!" Caroline and Maria called as Baxter pulled them out the door.

"Do you ever watch your dad's cross-country team?" Maria asked as Baxter dragged them along the sidewalk toward the park.

"No. He doesn't run any races — he's just the coach for a bunch of sweaty guys." Caroline wrinkled her nose. Once when she'd had a dentist appointment, her father had picked her up and taken her back to the high school with him. She had sat on the bleachers while the boys ran around the track. It was more boring than the documentaries her mother liked to watch on television.

"I love it when my mom takes me to the theater. When no one's looking, I sneak onto the stage and pretend I'm in a play." Maria did a few fancy dance steps and Baxter jumped up in the air, ready to play. "Did you see what Duncan drew today?" Maria asked.

"When?" Caroline hadn't noticed him drawing. But then, she had been careful to keep her eyes on her own paper to avoid any more disasters with Mrs. Nicks.

"During reading. He drew me." Maria giggled.

"What were you?"

Maria slipped her hands behind her neck and fluffed her long, wavy black hair. "I was a horse with a mane flying in the wind."

If Duncan had drawn a horse and labeled it Caroline, she would have thought he was saying she was big and clumsy. But Maria took it as a compliment.

"I'm thinking of letting my hair grow," Caroline told her friend.

"Really? How long?" Maria was instantly interested.

Caroline tried to stretch her hair. "I think it should be four inches longer by next summer if my mother doesn't make me cut it."

"Why would she do that?"

"Because long hair isn't *practical*. She says I can let it grow as long as I take care of it."

"Snarls are a pain." Maria sounded like someone who knew. "I get some *huge* knots in my hair."

"It would be worth it," Caroline said. "If Duncan draws me again, maybe I can be a horse like you."

"We could be twins!" Maria cried.

Caroline pulled on Baxter's leash to let him know it was time to go back to the house. "Yeah. Twin horses!"

When the house came into sight, Baxter broke away from Caroline and raced to the back porch. Laurie opened the door and the dog galloped inside. "Hello, Baxter. Have you brought the girls home?"

"We're here," Caroline called. She and Maria crowded into the kitchen. There was a big frying pan on the stove, and a bag of marshmallows and two cups full of breakfast cereal on the counter.

Laurie said, "The butter is melting in the pan. By the time you wash your hands, it'll be ready."

They both scrubbed their hands in the kitchen sink and then dried them on a dish-towel. Before they started cooking, Caroline hit a wooden spoon against the counter. "The Double Club will now come to order!"

They waited until the last bit of butter melt-ed. Then they counted out the marshmallows and took turns dropping them into the pan. Laurie had set out two spoons so they both could stir the marshmallows until they turned into white goo.

"Time for the cereal," Caroline called.

"Here you go." Laurie poured the cereal into the melted butter and marshmallows. It crackled as they put their spoons back into the pan and stirred. Laurie stood by until all the mixing was done. Then she scraped the gooey mixture into a flat pan to cool.

"Didn't we do it good?" Caroline asked proudly.

"It looks like a super job to me," Laurie

agreed. "We'll have to let it cool for a while. Why don't you girls watch some television in the family room? Isn't that throw-mud-on-your-face game show on now?"

"Yeah!" They scrambled into the family room next to the kitchen. Caroline turned on the television just in time to hear the host say, "Here's mud in your eye!"

Maria dropped into the easy chair where Mr. Zucker liked to rest at night. Caroline picked up one of the big pillows on the old couch and held it in her lap. When the host introduced the contestants, she groaned. "That one looks just like Duncan!"

"I hope someone smears him with mud," Maria said.

Caroline heard the back door open as her little sisters burst into the kitchen. She hoped Laurie wouldn't tell them where she and Maria were. After all, they were having a private club meeting.

When neither Patricia nor Vicki ran in, Caroline figured it was safe to talk. During a commercial, she told her friend, "I know you don't mind Duncan as much as I do, but he's really bothering me. He's making me look stupid in front of Michael."

"Oooh." Two little voices squealed from the doorway, and Caroline knew she had a problem.

"Get out of here!" she told her sisters.

"*Michael*," Patricia teased. "I want to know all about *Michael. . . .*"

". . . or I'll tell Mom," Vicki added, hugging Little Pillow, the battered old pillow she always dragged around with her. It didn't seem to matter to her that it was shedding feathers everywhere.

"They're so *cute*," Maria cooed. She was an only child.

"Cute?" Caroline shook her head. "You can take them home. Be my guest."

"I'm sorry, Caroline," Laurie said as she came into the room. She took the little girls' hands and said, "Let's find something more fun to do."

Caroline watched them leave. When they were out of sight, she stood up.

"Let's go up to my room until the crispy bars are cool enough to eat," she suggested. "I don't trust my sisters not to bug us again."

Maria ran up the stairs that led to the attic room. When she got to the top, she called, "You're so slow!"

"What's the big hurry?" Caroline asked, opening the door to her room.

"I think we should talk about my birthday." Maria walked into the room and waved at the goldfish in the bowl under the eaves.

"Birthday?" Caroline pretended to be surprised. "Do you have a birthday coming up?"

"In fifteen days."

"Then the Double Club should make a list of every single present in the world that you might want." Caroline dug in her desk drawer for a pad of paper and took a pen from the cup on top of it.

"A new bike would be nice," Maria said, stretching out on Caroline's bed. She picked up the pale blue stuffed rabbit by the pillow and tugged on his whiskers.

"One bike." Caroline made that the first thing on the list. "Any special color?"

"Chartreuse."

"What kind of color is that?" Caroline

asked. She had no idea how to spell it.

"It's a kind of yellowish green," Maria explained. "I'd also like a new radio, with speakers on each side that can come off. . . ."

As Caroline wrote down the details about the radio, her pen spit ink across the page. "Yuck!"

"What's wrong?" Maria sat up to make sure she wasn't missing anything.

"My pen died." She dropped it on the paper. "It's my favorite Denver Broncos pen."

"I've never seen it before," Maria said, still clutching the rabbit.

"I never took it to school because I knew Duncan would *borrow* it," Caroline told her. Suddenly an idea began forming in her mind.

"What if . . . " Her idea was absolutely wonderful! A real brainstorm! "What if I bring it to school next Monday and just kinda leave it sitting on my desk?"

"Duncan will steal it," Maria said. Then a light sparkled in her eyes. "He'll make a mess — "

"All over himself!" Caroline finished. "For

once, *we're* going to be the ones laughing."

"Ink all over Duncan Fairbush," Maria crowed. "I *love* it!"

5

EVERYONE LOVES CRISPY SQUARES

"Excuse me, ladies." Caroline's father stuck his head in the door of her room. She hadn't heard him come up the steps.

"Hi, Dad," Caroline cried.

"Hi, baby. Hello, Maria. I was coming up to let you know I was home when I thought I heard something about getting ink all over someone. . . ."

"Duncan. Duncan Fairbush," Caroline explained. "He deserves it!"

"He really does, Mr. Zucker," Maria said.

"What terrible things has Duncan the

41

Dreadful done now?" Caroline's dad asked.

"He's been drawing pictures. *Ugly* pictures. He puts my name on them and shows them to other people!" Caroline complained.

"Maybe he likes you."

Both girls stared at Mr. Zucker in astonishment. "Duncan Fairbush doesn't even like his own mother!" Caroline said.

Mr. Zucker came into the room. "I know it's hard for you to deal with Duncan, honey. But the smart way to handle him is to ignore him."

"How can I pretend he's not there when he makes the whole class laugh at me?" Caroline wailed.

"It won't be easy." Caroline's father took her small hand in his big one and gave it a squeeze. "But you're going to be the winner if you act more grown-up than he does. What do you say, Caroline?" Mr. Zucker let go of her hand and stood up.

Caroline decided not to tell her father she was still going to do the ink trick. Instead she gave him one of her best smiles, and asked, "Can we go to the Mile-High Diner tonight?"

"You know we can't go out tonight. We're eating at home and saving a plate for your mother."

"We could bring her something from Mile-High."

"Would it be fair for us to be having fun at dinner while your mother is working hard? We'll go out sometime when everyone is together."

Caroline sighed. "Okay. Mom would feel bad if she found out we'd gone to Mile-High without her."

When they heard Mr. Zucker going downstairs, Maria asked, "So are you still going to do it?" She pointed at the Broncos pen.

"Of course," Caroline said. "Dad just doesn't understand. I don't think he has anyone like Duncan in his classes."

"Do you think he draws pictures at home?" Maria wondered out loud.

"I bet he draws ugly pictures on the *walls*."

"And he invites people home to see them. . . ."

"Not Michael Hopkins!" The idea of Duncan showing more pictures of her that she had never even seen was scary. "I don't think Michael would go to Duncan's house."

Maria's stomach growled and she checked her watch. "Is this still the club meeting? It's four-thirty."

"Time for crispy squares!" Caroline beat her to the door and they raced down the stairs together.

When they burst into the kitchen, they saw Vicki staring at the counter. Laurie must have cut the treats into squares, because they were all stacked neatly on a plate. Vicki was so interested in the treats that she had actually dropped Little Pillow on the floor.

Caroline grabbed the dish as she announced, "This goes to the family room for the Double Club."

"Can't she have just one?" Maria asked, smiling down at Vicki.

"No."

"*I* would share if they were *mine*," Vicki said with a pout.

Maria took the top square off the stack and handed it to Vicki.

The little girl beamed. "Thank you."

"You're welcome," said Maria. She went into the family room to turn on the television, and Caroline squatted close to the floor.

"Vicki, come here," she said. Her sister came toward her slowly as if she half expected Caroline to take away her treat. Instead, Caroline handed two more squares to her sister and said, "One is for you and one is for Patricia." Vicki gave her a big kiss.

"Vicki, I told you I need the logs to be the same size," Caroline told her little sister an hour later. She picked up a skinny twig and held it next to a big fat one. "Do these look the same to you?"

Vicki pouted. "I just wanted to help."

Caroline held the two twigs against one side of the shoe box. "Do you see how they look? I have to cover the whole box with logs and it's not going to work if they're all so different. I'll give you another crispy square if you bring me some good logs."

Vicki didn't even take time to say good-bye. The back door slammed as she dashed into the yard.

"Mom's not going to like it when she finds out you cut up my blouse," Patricia warned as she handed Caroline some blue-and-white gingham.

"It's too small for you." Caroline wanted to use the fabric for checkered curtains.

"Mom would have given it to Vicki," Patricia insisted.

Caroline took the blouse out of Patricia's hands and showed her the black stain on the front. "No one could wear this blouse again after you let a black marker — one of *my* black markers — leak all over it!"

But before Caroline could cut curtains, she had to make windows. "Could you get me a sharp knife?" she asked Patricia.

"Sure." Patricia marched into the kitchen.

Caroline was outlining the windows when her father came back with Patricia. "Did you want a knife?" he asked.

"Yes." She held up the box. "I have to cut out the windows. If I use scissors, the edges will be all bumpy."

He nodded. "You're right. But I prefer not to leave a knife in here with you girls. What if I cut them out for you?"

"That would be great." Caroline wasn't sure she could get smooth-edged windows even with a knife. What if her hand shook?

Her father folded his long, long legs and sat on the floor with her. He made the cuts quickly. All three windows had even sides.

"Uh . . . want to do one more thing?" she asked.

"What do you have in mind?"

"The back door. I can't have a *front* door since the whole front of the cabin is open. So the back door has to be just right. . . ."

He picked up the knife again. "Where do you want this special door?"

She showed him the outline she had traced and he cut perfect lines. He even scored the cardboard along one side so the door would fold open easily.

Vicki trudged into the family room with her arms full of twigs and branches. "Are these enough?" she asked as she dropped them next to Caroline.

"What are these for?" their father asked.

"Logs. The Ingallses had a log cabin, so I

have to glue these on the outside of the box."

"Where's my crispy square?" Vicki wanted to know.

As Caroline went into the kitchen, her father was laughing. "It sure is interesting living in a house full of women. A guy could learn a lot about wheeling and dealing from you, Caroline Louise!"

6

ADVENTURES IN GROCERIES

"Can I drive?" Caroline liked grocery shopping, especially when she got to push the cart.

"If you promise not to run over any shoppers," Mrs. Zucker said, lifting Vicki and Little Pillow into the children's seat.

"No problem." Caroline raced down the first aisle.

"Wait!" her mother called. "I need to get some lettuce and potatoes."

They had to wait a minute to get close to the produce section. It seemed like everyone

49

shopping on Saturday morning needed potatoes. Once the bag was safely tucked in the
cart, they started down another aisle.

"Get the squeeze bottle, Mom," Caroline
suggested when her mother reached for pickle
relish.

"But it's more expensive. Do you want it to
be your treat?" Mrs. Zucker asked. When the
girls helped with grocery shopping, each got
to pick one thing for themselves. Caroline
knew if she chose the pickle relish, then she
couldn't get cookies or gum or even a sticker
book. But the idea of squeezing the pickle
relish out of the bottle was impossible to re-
sist. "I'll take it," she said.

"I want animal crackers," said Vicki. She
always got the same treat. "One for me and
one for Patricia."

"That's very nice of you to think of your
sister," Mrs. Zucker said.

"But Patricia isn't helping," Caroline pointed out.

"Patricia would be here if I hadn't decided to
do our shopping while she was at her piano
lesson," her mother explained.

"I'll give you one of my crackers," Vicki offered. "Do you want a camel or a tiger?"

"A tiger." When Vicki handed her *two* tiger crackers, Caroline smiled. Her littlest sister could be very generous. "Thanks. Next time we have hot dogs, you can use my pickle relish."

Vicki clapped her hands, squishing Little Pillow. Feathers flew into Caroline's face. She closed her eyes and as she did, she heard a very familiar voice.

"Hello, Mrs. Zucker."

Caroline kept her eyes closed, hoping she had imagined it.

"Why, Mrs. Nicks," her mother was saying. "It's nice to see you."

It isn't nice at all, Caroline thought to herself. What was she doing in the cereal aisle anyway? She inched the cart forward and whispered, "Mom, we have to hurry."

"Why?" her mother asked.

"Patricia's piano lesson will be over soon," Caroline said, still whispering.

"Your father is picking up Patricia." Her mother turned back to Mrs. Nicks and the

51

two women began to chat. How could her own mother be so friendly with the woman who hated her oldest daughter?

"I want some milk," Vicki whined.

"And I want to get out of here," Caroline told her. "But we have to wait for Mom to finish talking to my teacher."

"*That's* your teacher? The lady who doesn't like you?" Vicki turned her wide-eyed gaze on the woman talking to their mother. Vicki leaned close. "She looks mean. I'm glad my kindergarten teacher is nicer."

"I used to have nice teachers, too," Caroline said with a sigh. *Is that how it works?* she wondered. Do all the nice teachers take the little kids? And just when you really start to like school, do they think you're old enough to get the mean teachers? She hoped it wasn't true. It wouldn't be right if both Patricia and Vicki had to get third-grade teachers like Mrs. Nicks.

"How is your class working out this year?" she heard her mother ask Mrs. Nicks.

"It's a lively class," the teacher said with a laugh.

Mrs. Zucker laughed, too. "If you have many like my Caroline, I suppose you have your hands full."

Caroline's mouth fell open. They were acting like they were best friends or something!

"None of the girls causes much trouble," Mrs. Nicks said, and Caroline wondered if her teacher had forgotten about giving her detention last week. "But there are a couple of boys . . . well, let's just say I have a few more gray hairs than I used to."

"I'll see you at Open School Night," Mrs. Zucker told the teacher, and Caroline got ready to get the cart rolling again. She watched her mother get a drum of oatmeal, and behind her Mrs. Nicks reached to the top shelf for a big box of Yummy Bites. Caroline had heard Mrs. Nicks didn't have any children or grandchildren. So why was she getting a cereal that Caroline's father liked to call "Captain Cavity?" Someone should tell her that kind of thing wasn't good for her.

Caroline's parents were on the couch in the family room. Her dad was watching a mystery show on television while her mother read. Vicki was lying on the floor at her mother's feet with Little Pillow. Patricia was sitting in a chair with a comic book.

Just in case anyone was interested, Caroline lifted up her diorama so they could all see the windows. She had worked hard to stretch clear plastic food wrap tightly across the open squares so her windows wouldn't be wrinkly. The tape showed around the edges, but she would cover it with the curtains she had made.

Her mother glanced up from her nursing magazine. "It's looking good. Are other people in your class making dioramas too?"

"Most kids are doing boring book reports instead." Caroline jumped up and headed toward the kitchen. She called back to her family, "It's time for me to see if my curtain rods are ready."

"I want to see, too." Patricia followed her.

Caroline touched the thin sticks sitting on a paper towel on the counter. They were stiff and dry. No one would ever guess she had made them by soaking string in a salt and water mixture. "Now I can glue the curtains to them and hang them in the cabin."

"I want to help," Vicki said, running into the kitchen.

"No. You might wreck something." Caroline carefully carried the two sticks into the next room. While her sisters watched, she glued the curtains onto the rods and then used her father's special heavy-duty paste to attach the whole thing to her windows.

"It's so pretty," Vicki said, running her fingers along the outside of the box.

"Don't do that!" Caroline swatted at her sister's hand. "What if the logs come off?"

"I helped find them." Vicki rocked back on her heels and pouted.

"And I gave up my blouse for the curtains, but did I get to help hang them?" Patricia answered her own question. "Of course not."

"Caroline," her mother called. "Try to be more patient with your sisters. And Patricia and Vicki, don't bother her when she's working so hard on a school project."

Caroline sat back to admire her work. The windows were perfect. Now she'd have to start on the furniture. She could make a trundle bed out of cardboard and construction paper. And there were scraps in her mother's sewing basket just right for a quilt. Maria had offered to lend her a miniature rocking chair from her dollhouse for the big room. The only real problem left was the cook stove.

"It's getting late," Mr. Zucker announced.

Caroline set her diorama inside a large cardboard box and slipped her extra supplies into a paper sack. Carefully balancing the bag on top of the box, she started to leave the room.

"Can we trust you girls to get ready for bed by yourselves?" Mrs. Zucker asked.

"We'll be fine, Mom," Caroline said.

After their parents promised to come upstairs for good-night hugs and kisses, the girls trotted through the kitchen. Patricia looked from Caroline to Vicki. "Wouldn't it be fun to have a pillow fight with Little Pillow?"

"No!" Vicki ran toward her room to protect her best buddy. Little Pillow could lose what little stuffing he had left in a fight.

Patricia's blue eyes sparkled. "Let's get her!"

"As soon as I put away my diorama," Caroline said. After she tucked the box in her closet, she'd grab her own pillow and head for Vicki's room. They wouldn't really hurt Vicki's little friend. But they'd have a great pillow fight! Who said sisters weren't fun?

7

HERE'S INK IN YOUR FACE

Caroline glanced across the aisle to check on Maria. She was looking over her shoulder at Caroline. Maria winked.

For a while, Caroline hadn't been sure Monday would ever come. But they had been in school for two hours now and she could hardly sit still in her seat.

Caroline slid her hand inside her desk to touch the leaky Broncos pen. It was ready. They were really going to get Duncan! All they were waiting for was the right time.

"How many of you have finished your writing assignment?" Mrs. Nicks asked the class.

Caroline raised her hand. She knew her paper wasn't very neat, but Mrs. Nicks had not asked who had copied the poem with perfect printing.

Since only five other kids had finished, the teacher decided, "Let's take another fifteen minutes on the project. Those of you who have finished should get something from the Enrichment Box."

Maria looked over her shoulder at Caroline and mouthed, "This is it." While Caroline dug around in the box for an interesting extra-credit math game, Duncan could be making a mess of himself with her pen.

Careful not to attract any attention, she opened her desk just enough to slide out the pen. She held it by the top so she wouldn't get any ink on herself, and then she set it on her desk. Now she just had to give Duncan a chance to take it.

Caroline stood up and started to walk toward the front of the aisle. She should have kept an eye on Duncan Fairbush, but she didn't. His foot shot out in front of her, and Caroline tripped over it and fell against Maria.

"Forget how to walk?" he said softly, so only she and Maria heard him.

Caroline bit her lower lip, determined to say nothing. She stood and brushed imaginary lint off her jeans. Then she went to the shelf by the window. It wasn't easy going through the box while she was trying to watch her desk. Why wasn't Duncan turning around the way he usually did? Wasn't he going to notice the pen?

Just then, Duncan twisted around in his seat, and Caroline could see his nasty grin when he spotted her Broncos pen. He looked around to make sure no one was watching him (he didn't see Caroline spying on him from across the room). Then he snatched the pen.

Caroline quickly flipped through the packets and found the one she wanted. As she headed back to her row, she saw him begin to doodle with her pen. It was hard for her not to laugh out loud when the blue ink squirted out and made a big blue splotch on his shirt.

Maria was watching him, too. Caroline

could see her friend's dark eyes sparkling. She slowed her steps so she could enjoy all of Duncan's disaster. Sitting behind him, she might miss part of it.

When he flipped the pen over to see what was wrong with it, ink smeared on both of his hands. And then something happened that was even better than she'd hoped for. His nose must have started to itch, because he rubbed his face and left a blue mustache.

"Look at Duncan!" someone called out.

One by one, everyone turned to stare. Kids in the back of the room stood up to get a better view. Everyone laughed. Caroline was fascinated by the way Duncan's face turned red. Under the blue ink around his mouth, he looked purple. The laughter got louder and louder.

Now Duncan had to know how awful she felt every time he made fun of her. And he didn't seem to like it any better than she did.

"Geez, Caroline," he finally said. "Are you so poor you can't buy a good pen?"

Immediately, she felt her own face heating up, and she hurried back to her seat. But he wasn't finished with her.

"I mean, I borrowed your pen and look what it did to me!" He handed it back to her, making sure she got ink on her hands.

"Duncan!" Mrs. Nicks called. "Would you like a pass to the rest room so you can clean up?"

"Sure." He walked up to her desk and leaned against it while she filled out his pass.

"Where did you get such a stupid pen, Zucker?" Kevin called from the back of the room.

Caroline swallowed hard. Her father had bought the pen for her at a Broncos game last year and she'd loved using it until it sprang a leak. Refusing to answer, she stared down at her desk.

"What's wrong with The Zuck?" Duncan asked from the front of the room.

The Zuck? Caroline hated that nickname even more than Yucker.

Maria sent her a sympathetic glance. It was a pretty sad scene. Caroline had been so excited about their plan to trick Duncan and he had turned it all back on her. Every day, he seemed to get worse. What more could he do to make her life miserable?

Caroline didn't get a chance to talk to Maria until lunch. They huddled together at the end of the line.

"I can't *believe* what happened!" Maria put a hand on Caroline's shoulder.

"I wish I could go home and crawl under my bed," Caroline told her friend.

"What can I do to cheer you up?" Maria asked.

Sadly, Caroline said, "Nothing will help. I tried to think about my great diorama and even that couldn't make me feel better."

They stayed at the end of the line as the class moved into the hall. "Do you still need the rocking chair?" Maria asked.

"Yeah."

"I'll bring it over after school. My mom will be home, and I think she'll give me a ride."

"Maybe you can stay for dinner at my house." Caroline wanted someone around who would understand what a bad day she'd had at school. "My dad will take you home afterward."

"I'll ask."

By the time the end of the line reached the lunch counter, the chicken nuggets were gone. Instead, the kitchen helpers put day-old spaghetti and slippery peach slices on their plates.

When they found two places at a table, Maria shook her head. "I didn't like the spaghetti *yesterday.*"

"I know." Caroline sighed. "It seems like everything is going wrong today."

"Hey, The Zuck has lost her appetite!" Duncan hollered as he passed their table.

"He probably hopes he can get me to starve to death," Caroline said grimly.

"Or maybe he's hoping you'll throw your plate at him and get in big trouble with the cafeteria monitor."

"Maybe The Zuck would rather have some chicken. Do you want mine?" Michael Hopkins waved a nugget in the air.

Under normal circumstances, Caroline would have been thrilled if Michael had offered to share his lunch with her. But he had actually called her The Zuck!

She couldn't stay there for another minute. She jumped off the bench and ran for the door. Maria was right behind her. When the monitor came toward them, Caroline covered her mouth with one hand and pretended she was going to be sick.

"I'm her friend. I have to help her," Maria said.

Caroline kept running until she reached the rest room. When Maria came through the swinging door, Caroline leaned against the cool tile wall.

"Did you hear it?" she moaned. "Did you hear Michael call me The Zuck?"

"Duncan Fairbush has gone too far." Maria's dark eyes were flashing. She was truly angry. "Caroline Zucker, you are the best planner in the whole school. We are going to figure out some way to make him sorry he ever messed with you."

Maria was right. Between them, Caroline was sure they would think of something to make Duncan sorry he had ever started fooling around with Caroline Louise Zucker.

8

THANK YOU, TERRIBLE TONY

"I'm so glad your mom let you come over today," Caroline told Maria later that same afternoon. They were walking to the park.

Maria pushed her long hair, blown by the breeze, out of her face. "We need to plan."

Caroline added, "And my sisters won't be hanging around the park to listen."

"Or your dad. We don't want him to hear us either," Maria said.

The park was nearly empty, and the girls headed for the swings. Caroline sat on one and Maria took the swing next to her.

"This is a perfect place to talk about Duncan," Caroline said.

"I've got it!" Maria exclaimed. "We could sneak into his house and leave plastic spiders in his bed."

Caroline laughed at the idea, but they wouldn't be there to see it, so that was no good. "What if we put them in the water fountain just before Duncan gets a drink?"

"Or we could bake him some brownies with tomato sauce in the recipe," Maria said with a wide grin. "He'd eat them all during lunch and then he'd be scratching like crazy all afternoon."

"And we could watch!" Caroline liked the idea of seeing him squirm.

Maria pushed off and let herself swing. "And the *best* part is that he would know exactly who did it to him." Then she put down her feet and came to a jolting stop. "Wait. It won't work. The brownies wouldn't taste right with tomato sauce in them. He wouldn't eat them."

Caroline stopped swinging, too. "You're probably right. Then we'll just have to trick him into doing something really embarrassing."

"Like what?" Maria wrapped her arms around the swing chains and then let her body fall forward. "Can we make him call Mrs. Nicks 'Dog Face?'"

"That would be pretty bad, wouldn't it?" Caroline chuckled when she imagined the look on their teacher's face. "What if we kept hiding his science and social studies books? You know, a different place every day?"

"But we might get in trouble if we got caught," Maria pointed out. "*Us* getting into trouble isn't part of the plan."

"Of course not. Only Dreadful Duncan Fairbush is supposed to be embarrassed. . . ." Caroline sprang off her swing. "I've got it!"

Her friend was right behind her. "What is it? What's the plan?"

Caroline said eagerly, "What's the name of the book you're doing your report on? The one about the boy who gets into so much trouble?"

"*Terrible Tony Thompson,*" Maria said. "My favorite part is when Tony strings a cord across the door and trips that snobby girl when she comes into the classroom."

Caroline asked, "Doesn't that sound like something Duncan might do? Something we could *help* him do, and make sure he gets caught?"

"I like your idea!" Maria grinned for a minute. Then she asked, "How?"

Caroline sat on the bench. "We have to put the idea into his head and then make sure he acts out the scene."

Maria shrugged her shoulders. "Sounds hard."

"Not really." Caroline had a plan. "What if he heard us talking about it? You could tell me all about the story, and then we'd laugh about your favorite scene. You know he'll eavesdrop on us."

Maria grinned and nodded. "He always does. He's nosy *and* mean."

"One of us will have to bring the supplies," Caroline said, getting practical. "I mean, he's not going to have a cord with him."

Maria nodded. "I'll bring one. I can talk about Tony's trick. And then I'll tell you how strange it is that I have a piece of cord in my desk." Then she frowned. "Who'll trip over the cord? Will someone get hurt?"

Caroline frowned, too. She didn't want anyone to really get hurt. But if the person already *knew* the cord would be strung across the door, then he or she could just pretend to fall over it. "That's it! I'll get out of class somehow, and then I'll be the one who falls."

Maria said, "Now there's only one thing left — making sure Duncan gets blamed!" Her dark eyes sparkled. "When he's not looking, I'll sneak an extra piece of cord into his desk."

"Evidence!" Caroline clapped her hands. "This is great!"

"When should we do it? Tomorrow?" Maria asked.

But they had just tried the pen trick that morning. "He might be suspicious if we try it too soon."

"I guess we should wait a few days," Maria agreed.

Caroline stood on the bench and tugged on Maria's arm until her friend jumped up beside her. "Friday. Duncan Fairbush doesn't know it, but he's going to get into *tons* of trouble on Friday!"

She began jumping up and down. Maria joined her. Together they counted to three and then leaped off the bench into the children's sand pit. Together they screamed, *"Friday!"*

Caroline opened and closed the shutters on the bedroom window of her shoe box cabin. The brown construction paper wasn't very heavy, so she planned to leave the shutters closed. That way they wouldn't rip off when she took the diorama to school the next day.

Maria's miniature rocking chair looked perfect in the big room. The cook stove hadn't turned out as well as she had hoped, but no one would notice it was slightly off-balance when they saw the orange paper fire inside it. At first, the paper flames had looked even sadder than the stove itself. Then she remembered the orange glitter her mother had bought for making Halloween decorations. Now the flames sparkled when they caught the light.

"Mom? Don't you think my diorama is good?" Caroline asked when her mother came into the kitchen.

Her mother sat down at the table to study the project. "I love the stove with the fire in it."

"Did you see the woodbox behind the stove?" Caroline had filled it with the tiniest twigs that Vicki had gathered.

"I bet no one else in your class has done a diorama as good as this one," her mother said, trying out the shutters in the bedroom. "What is Maria's like?"

"She's just writing a book report."

"So Mrs. Nicks gave you a choice between doing a report or making a diorama?" Mrs. Zucker asked.

Caroline said, "Actually, she told us all to write book reports."

Her mother gently closed the shutters. "Then why have you spent hours doing this? Is it extra credit?"

"Not exactly . . . "

Mrs. Zucker sighed. "You didn't write a book report, did you?"

"No . . . " Caroline kept busy checking each

of the twigs she'd glued to the outside of the box. She would hate to have any of them fall off on the way to school.

"Do you think Mrs. Nicks will be happy with your diorama?"

"Oh, yes!" Caroline exclaimed. "She'll love my project. When she gets tired of reading all the boring book reports, she can look at my diorama!"

"I hope you're right," her mother said in a tone that hinted she wasn't at all sure.

"I *am* right. Tomorrow is going to be my best day in third grade!"

Caroline went up to her room, but she was too excited to sleep. "Hey, Justin and Esmerelda. Are you awake?" she asked her goldfish. Justin wiggled his tail and swam around in circles.

Caroline sat cross-legged on the edge of her bed and rubbed her hands together. "Tomorrow, Mrs. Nicks will know how smart I am. And Friday — in just three days — Duncan Fairbush is going to find out how dangerous it is to mess around with me!"

9

"D" IS FOR DIORAMA . . . AND DISASTER!

"What's in your bag?" Samantha Collins asked in class the next morning, eyeing the big shopping bag in Caroline's hand.

"Nothing," Caroline answered. She wasn't going to tell anyone about her diorama. She wanted it to be a big surprise.

"The Zuck brought an empty bag to class!" Duncan announced, standing on his chair.

Caroline wanted to tell him to laugh all he wanted, because he wouldn't be laughing on Friday. But she didn't.

She put the shopping bag under her desk

and tucked her feet under her chair. The diorama had made it to school safely — she didn't want to break it by accidentally kicking it.

"Does everyone have their book reports?" Mrs. Nicks asked the class.

Some kids groaned, but most of them said their reports were ready. Caroline nodded her head. Mrs. Nicks had warned she might call on some of them to tell the class about the books they'd read. Caroline hoped she would be chosen. Then she could hold her diorama up for the whole class to admire.

"Kevin," the teacher said, "would you tell us about your book?"

Kevin carried his rumpled paper to the front of the class. "I read *Barky Wins the Game*. It's about this dog who plays baseball . . . "

Caroline let herself think about her diorama. It had turned out even better than she'd expected.

"Susan," the teacher called when Kevin went back to his desk.

"My report is about *Monica Baby-Sits*." Every boy in the class laughed out loud, and

Susan refused to look up from her paper. She read it aloud very fast, then hurried back to her desk.

By the time three other kids had told about their books, Caroline was starting to think she wouldn't get a chance to show off her project.

"Caroline, would you like to share your report with us?" Mrs. Nicks finally asked.

Would she like to? She'd love to!

Caroline grasped the bag by its handles and pulled it from beneath her desk. She marched to the front of the class with her head held high. Setting the bag on the chair next to the teacher's desk, she gently lifted the diorama out of its tissue-paper wrappings.

"I read *Little House in the Big Woods* by Laura Ingalls Wilder," she told the class. "I thought it would be interesting to make a diorama of the cabin where the Ingalls family lived, so that's what I did."

She showed them the big room with the fire in the cook stove. Then she pointed out the small bedroom where the whole family slept, and the attic where the girls had played on

Book Reports due
Today !

days when they could not be outside.

Mrs. Nicks bent down to inspect the windows and the "logs" on the cabin. Just as Caroline had expected, her teacher was very impressed. She said, "The diorama is wonderful. You were very clever to make the pioneer cabin come to life."

Caroline smiled so hard that her face hurt. Even in her dreams, she had not imagined how good it would be to hear Mrs. Nicks praise her. She felt all warm inside. Things were going to change, she just knew it! School was going to be as much fun as it had been last year and the year before.

"But Caroline, where is your book report?" Mrs. Nicks was asking.

"Book report?" Caroline blinked, trying to understand the question. "This *is* my book report."

Mrs. Nicks leaned back against her desk and pursed her lips. She didn't really look angry; it was more like she was disappointed. "The book report was a *writing* assignment," Mrs. Nicks explained. "Your diorama is an impressive extra-credit project, but I still need to have a book report from you."

"But . . ." Caroline sucked on her bottom lip. It wasn't fair! She had worked harder on the diorama than Kevin had on his baseball dog report. Didn't all the details in the cabin prove she had read the book?

"What if I give you another week to get it done?"

In the back of her mind, Caroline knew the teacher was being very fair. But she didn't want to *write* a book report. If she'd wanted to write one, she would have.

"Can you give me a book report on *Little House in the Big Woods* by next Friday?"

Caroline swallowed twice to get the lump out of her throat. "Sure," she squeaked.

"The Zuck is going to cry!" Duncan sounded very pleased. There was no way she was going to cry and make him even happier. Caroline squared her shoulders and marched back to her desk. When Duncan spun around to bother her some more, she ignored him.

"That's all the time we have for sharing," Mrs. Nicks announced. "Please pass your reports forward."

The person behind her tapped Caroline on the shoulder. She took the papers and passed them to Duncan.

"Too bad you don't have a report," he said.

I'll have a report, Caroline promised herself. *And my report will be better than anything Duncan Fairbush could ever write.* Caroline Zucker was going to prove to Mrs. Nicks once and for all that she was one of the best students in the class. And she was finally going to get the attention she deserved!

10

OUTSMARTING DUNCAN FAIRBUSH

"I read the neatest story for my book report," Maria told Caroline in a loud whisper after lunch on Friday.

"What was it?" Caroline saw Duncan twist toward the aisle, and she knew he was listening. They would have to work fast — the class was ready to break into reading groups.

Maria giggled. *"Terrible Tony Thompson."*

"I read that!" Caroline lied. "Didn't you *love* the scene where he strung the cord in the doorway to trip that nasty girl?"

With her dark eyes open wider than usual,

Maria said, "Oh, yes! I laughed so hard when she tripped and fell into the room." She paused and glanced in Duncan's direction and then back at Caroline. "You know what? I have a piece of cord in my desk. . . ."

"You do?"

Maria lifted her desk top a tiny bit and showed Caroline the end of the cord. Then she left the cord hanging over the edge of the desk when she closed it.

Mrs. Nicks coughed and then asked, "Is everyone prepared for reading groups?"

The teacher's aide who always helped with reading hadn't come to their room yet. So Mrs. Nicks was going to be very, very busy. Caroline and Maria could not have picked a better time.

Maria slid out of her desk chair and joined her group on the other side of the room. Duncan didn't move from his desk until Caroline walked to the front of the room. Out of the corner of her eye, she saw him inching toward Maria's desk. He was going to do it!

"Mrs. Nicks? Could I have a pass for the rest room?" Caroline asked innocently.

"But it's time for reading."

"I won't take long." She made a desperate face and pretended she was having a real emergency.

"Oh, all right." Mrs. Nicks scribbled her initials on a small slip of paper and handed it to Caroline.

Caroline hurried around the corner and went into the girls's bathroom. Since she had to give Duncan time to string the cord while Mrs. Nicks was busy helping one of the reading groups, she'd have to wait around for a while.

Just then, Caroline heard footsteps in the hall. When the unseen person coughed, she realized that Mrs. Nicks was out there. Her teacher was spending a long time at the fountain.

Caroline suddenly gasped. Unless she could get back to the room before Mrs. Nicks, the teacher would fall over the cord instead of her! What if she got hurt? Mrs. Nicks was already returning to the classroom. Caroline could hear her high heels clicking on the floor.

"Oh, no," she whispered as she followed her

teacher around the corner and saw Mrs. Nicks with her hand on the doorknob.

Duncan had had enough time to rig the cord. Caroline knew she could call out and warn her, but then the teacher would blame her for the trick. And that would ruin everything. *Duncan* was the one who was supposed to get caught.

While Caroline wondered what she should do, Mrs. Nicks opened the door and took one step into the room. Then she tripped. Caroline covered her mouth with both hands, expecting something terrible to happen. But the teacher just stumbled over the cord, regaining her balance quickly.

Caroline heard the whole class erupt with laughter. She ran into the room, careful to step over the cord. Duncan had tied one end to a chair next to the door and the other to one of the cabinets on the other side of the doorway.

Duncan Fairbush was very worried now. First he sat at his desk, but he was too nervous to stay there. Then he stood up and wiped his sweaty hands on his jeans. When

85

Mrs. Nicks glared at him, he sat down again. And then he was back on his feet in a few seconds.

Caroline laughed. "Duncan looks like a yo-yo. Up and down, up and down."

The class started laughing all over again, and it was clear Mrs. Nicks had not appreciated her comment. The teacher was sitting behind her desk with her hands folded in front of her. Caroline knew Mrs. Nicks was very angry, but she couldn't help it if everyone thought she was funny.

"A yo-yo?" Kevin asked.

"A Duncan yo-yo," Michael announced.

Pretty soon, everyone had something to say.

"Hey, Duncan yo-yo, have you been around the world lately?"

"No, he's been walking the dog!"

"But does he glow in the dark?"

It seemed there were hundreds of yo-yo jokes once the class got started. But Mrs. Nicks lost her patience and pounded on her desk with her tape dispenser.

"Duncan!" Mrs. Nicks stared at him with steely eyes. "Was this trick in the doorway your idea?"

"I guess so."

"You guess so? What is that supposed to mean?" she demanded.

"Umm . . . "

Mrs. Nicks wasn't willing to wait for him to make up his mind. "Tell the truth, Duncan."

"It was my idea," he mumbled.

"Then we'll be spending some time together next week. Detention every day."

"Aw, Mrs. Nicks," he complained.

"Would you rather see the principal?" she asked.

"No." He slumped into his chair.

"It seems that our reading time is over," Mrs. Nicks told the class. People groaned, pretending to be sorry. "Please turn to page twenty in your social studies books."

Caroline was just opening her book when Duncan spun around in his seat. He didn't say anything. He just looked at her. She was surprised by his new expression. He wasn't laughing at her. He wasn't acting as if he was smarter than she was. He was impressed. And Caroline could tell he wasn't going to mess with her again for a very long time.

When she looked at Maria, her friend nodded toward the other side of the room. Caroline saw Michael Hopkins smiling at her. Michael wouldn't be calling her The Zuck again.

"Caroline?"

She snapped to attention when Mrs. Nicks called her name. "Yes?"

"I just asked you to explain what a community is," Mrs. Nicks said.

"It's . . . a bunch of people?"

Samantha Collins giggled over the silly answer, and Caroline laughed, too. Social studies didn't seem very important that afternoon. She had finally gotten even with Duncan! Duncan's yo-yo act was better than anything she could have planned.

"Thanks," Caroline whispered to the back of his head.

Duncan looked over his shoulder and asked, "For what?"

She gave him a great big grin. "For making this one of the best days of my life!"

* * *

"I can get *anything* I want?" Caroline asked her parents that night at the Mile-High Diner. They had already given her two dollars to spend on video games, and now they had handed her a menu.

"Anything. As long as you'll eat every bite," her father said.

"Honey, we know dinner won't make up for your disappointment over your English project. . . ." Although her mother didn't finish her comment, Caroline knew what she meant. Her parents were trying to let her know how much they loved her. How many other kids could say they had such nice families?

"I know you'll do a good job on your book report," her mother told her.

"I plan to do a better report than anyone in my class," Caroline announced. It wouldn't be hard doing better than Kevin Sutton, she told herself.

Her father smiled. "That's an impressive goal."

"I have to show Mrs. Nicks I'm one of the best students in the class."

"Why didn't your teacher like your diorama?" Patricia wanted to know.

"It was pretty," Vicki said, shredding a napkin, since their parents had not allowed Little Pillow to go out to dinner with them.

"She did like it," Caroline told them. "She thought it was really good and she's going to give me extra credit. She just said I had to write a real book report, too."

"We'll help you," Patricia announced. "I'll try not to practice the piano while you're working on your assignment," she offered.

Vicki added, "And I'll let you use Little Pillow whenever you need him."

Caroline smiled at everyone, hoping she'd always remember how good she felt at that very moment. "Thanks. It will be nice to have your help, Patricia."

"What about me?" Vicki asked with concern.

"You and Little Pillow?" She patted her youngest sister on the head. "He's *your* special friend. If I took him, he would miss you. If I get too lonely . . . well, you can just give me a hug."

Vicki threw her arms around her big sister right there in the restaurant. "I love you, Caroline."

"I love you, too." She was too shy to tell each person in her family how much she cared about them, but she got a strong feeling they already knew.

"You know something?" Caroline's father asked her mother. "It's not so bad being the only man in the family when all the ladies are as special as the four of you."

All Caroline could do was smile. If she could pick her own family, she would choose the very same parents — and even Patricia and Vicki. They were the best family in the whole wide world!